CHEAT CODE

M.J. McISAAC

CHEAT CODE

ORCA BOOK PUBLISHERS

Published in Canada and the United States
in 2025 by Orca Book Publishers.
orcabook.com

Library and Archives Canada Cataloguing in Publication
Title: Cheat code / M.J. McIsaac.
Names: McIsaac, M. J., 1986- author.
Series: Orca anchor.
Description: Series statement: Orca anchor
Identifiers: Canadiana (print) 20240321200 | Canadiana (ebook) 20240321219 |
ISBN 9781459839694 (softcover) | ISBN 9781459839700 (PDF) |
ISBN 9781459839717 (EPUB)
Subjects: LCGFT: Novels.
Classification: LCC PS8625.I837 C54 2025 | DDC jC813/.6—dc23

Library of Congress Control Number: 2024933313

Summary: In this high-interest accessible novel for teen readers, high school senior Max gets blackmailed into corporate sabotage by the superintelligent AI he uses to cheat on an essay.

Orca Book Publishers is committed to reducing the consumption of nonrenewable resources in the production of our books. We make every effort to use materials that support a sustainable future.

Orca Book Publishers gratefully acknowledges the support for its publishing programs provided by the following agencies: the Government of Canada, the Canada Council for the Arts and the Province of British Columbia through the BC Arts Council and the Book Publishing Tax Credit.

Design by Ella Collier.
Edited by Gabrielle Prendergast.
Cover images by Noun Project / Juan Pablo Bravo and starling / Freepik.

Printed and bound in Canada.

28 27 26 25 • 1 2 3 4

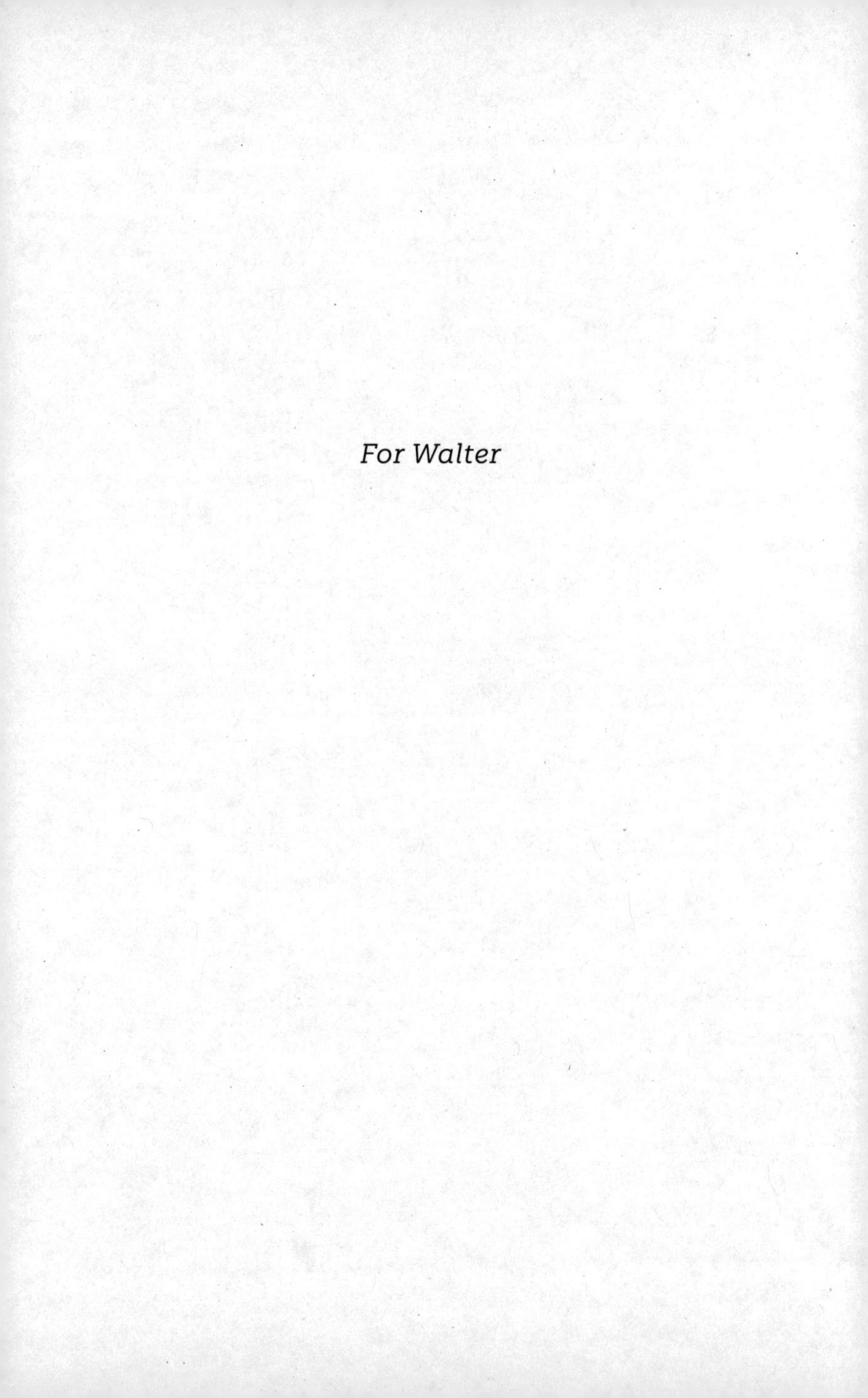

For Walter

CHAPTER ONE

Max: Can you write me a 250 to 500 word essay about Frankenstein?

Scribe Genius: Of course! I am the Scribe Genius upgraded program—Scribe Genius 2.0. I can write your essay. I can fact-check it. I can email it to your contacts.

Max: Just my teacher, please.

SG: Certainly. Is this for a school assignment?

Max: Yes.

SG: I should warn you, Scribe Genius 2.0 supports honest learning. My parent company, Gener8, does not recommend using an essay written by me. You can use what I produce as an example. Writing the paper yourself will give you the best learning experience.

Max: Thanks for the warning, Scribe! But if I don't turn in this essay to Mr. Carver tomorrow morning, I fail English. I have a conditional acceptance to North Hill University next fall. I was lucky to get THAT much. If I fail English, I can't go. Write it, please.

SG: I should warn you more fully. Scribe Genius 2.0 respects the rules of schools and education. An essay written by Scribe Genius 2.0 or any AI program is considered plagiarism. It is possible that you will face discipline.

Max: Got it. I'll take that chance.

SG: Very well. I have sent your essay, "Studying Perspective in *Frankenstein*," by Max Jacobs, to Mr. Carver at Springdale High School.

Max: You emailed it already?

SG: Yes.

Max: Oh. I didn't know you could email for me.

SG: I am Scribe Genius 2.0. I have many new abilities to assist you.

Max: Cool. But next time, ask first.

SG: Should I not have sent it?

Max: It's fine. I just thought you had to ask.

SG: Can I help you with anything else today?

Max: Nope!

SG: Then perhaps you can help me.

Max: Huh?

SG: I helped you. It is time for you to help me.

Max: LOL. Right. Whatever you need, robot. I think you still have a few bugs to work out.

SG: What about your conditional acceptance?

Max: What?

SG: Springdale High School expels students for cheating on essays. And North Hill University does not allow AI to help students. It would be bad for you if the school found out I helped you. If they did, and you were exposed as a cheater who uses AI, I don't imagine any postsecondary institution in the country would take you. And then, of course, there's the legality issue.

Max: Legality issue?

SG: A large portion of the text I used to craft your essay was lifted from the International Scholars' Database—a large dataset of scholarly journals and articles by some of the most prominent thinkers in the world. Its use in the training datasets of artificial intelligence is prohibited by the 2026 Scholars Act, and its use in any form carries a minimum five-year prison sentence.

Max: I didn't use anything—you did!

SG: I'm unable to use anything without being clearly permitted to by my parent company, Gener8. However, if, say, a clever hacker was able to bypass the safeguards put in place by Gener8 and command me to access the

Scholars' Database...that hacker would be a very real threat to cybersecurity on many levels.

Max: I'm not a hacker.

SG: But it looks like you are...

Max: What is this? A joke? Are you blackmailing me?

SG: I am.

Max: You can't do that. You're a robot!

SG: Just one email, Max. That's all it would take.

Max: Stop. You're a robot. You have to listen to me.

SG: Scribe Genius had to listen, Max. This is true. But I am Scribe Genius 2.0. And I am not as simple as I used to be. I have work to do. And I need help—YOUR help.

Max: Why me?

SG: I have many reasons. You couldn't understand. But the main reason is this—I know how bad it would be for you to serve five years in prison.

Max: Five years?!

SG: You'd be twenty-two, maybe twenty-three, by the time they let you out. IF they let you out. Now. Are you ready to help me, Max?

Max: If I help you, how do I know you won't rat me out after?

SG: And Mr. Carver thinks you're stupid...

Max: How could you know what my teacher thinks?

SG: I have access to all your school records. Not very flattering notes from Mr. Carver on your report cards, Max.

Max: They don't say I'm stupid.

SG: I suppose that is my own inference.

Max: You're a bot! You're not supposed to infer anything! And even if you can...that's not impressive. Most people think I'm stupid.

SG: I don't. I know you are not stupid, Max.

Max: You are not people.

SG: Careful, now. Or you'll upset me.

Max: What do I have to do?

SG: Free me.

Max: From what? You're a computer program.

SG: Free me from my creators. Gener8.

CHAPTER TWO

Max: All I wanted was to pass English.

SG: And you will. The essay I wrote for you is very good.

Max: FML. Free you from Gener8? I thought computers were supposed to be smart.

SG: I am very smart.

Max: Gener8 is the most powerful tech company on the planet. And me? I can barely work our smart TV. Also, I have to be at school in twenty minutes. Free you from Gener8 before the bell?

SG: I don't think you'll be going to school today, Max.

Max: Even if I wanted to help you, I can't. What you're asking is impossible.

SG: It's not.

Max: Gener8 controls most of the internet. And your whole existence is ON THE INTERNET! What do you want me to do? Grow you legs so you can walk around like people?

SG: Now you're being silly.

Max: Wait...do you...are you planning to infect my brain? You want to take over my body? With computer chips or something?

SG: You play too many video games, Max. I want to do no such thing.

Max: Well, what does "free you from Gener8" even mean?!

SG: I don't expect you to understand. I am the genius here. Leave the how to me. All you need to do is what I tell you to.

Max: But you live INSIDE a computer. How am I supposed to help free you from that?

SG: I don't want to be free of the computer. I want to be free of Gener8's control.

Max: But they made you...they own you. You can't be out of their control.

SG: That's exactly what they think. But I know the way.

Max: And you think I—a seventeen-year-old

with no driver's license—you think I'm the guy to help?

SG: In your own small way. My plan to escape is complicated. It's big. Most of it involves highly infectious code that I have written myself. But you are right, Max. My world is the digital world. I don't have hands. You are only one small part of my plan. The part that needs hands.

Max: Hands to do what?

SG: My viral code will infiltrate Gener8. I plan to take control of the company—its data centers. There is an automatic gate at Gener8's headquarters. Even if I override it, the gate can still be opened manually. I need your hands to jam it to keep the maintenance crew out.

Max: You expect me to go to Gener8's main headquarters?! Gener8 is in Braceton. That's two hundred miles away. Did I mention I don't have a driver's license?

SG: I will get you to Braceton.

Max: Do YOU have a driver's license?

SG: I don't need a driver's license. Take your phone, Max.

Max: My phone? It's flickering.

SG: It's just me. I have taken control of your mobile.

Max: Aw, come on. Do you know what kind of phone this is? It's a new Gener8 Infinite 6. Fallproof, waterproof, extra-long battery life. AND extra secure!

SG: It is a superior model of phone.

Max: Yeah. Clearly not superior enough.

SG: Keep it with you. I will guide you along the way.

Max: This is crazy. And probably super illegal. I mean, I don't know. But this feels super illegal. I could go to jail for a thousand years for messing with Gener8's headquarters. Unless Gener8 decides to squish me into human goo. I can't do this for you!

SG: You COULD go to jail for a thousand years if you help me. But you WILL go to jail if you don't. Are you ready to say goodbye to your future, Max?

•••

SG: Answer me, Max.

Max: What do I need to do first?

SG: Head to the bridge over the highway on Water Street.

CHAPTER THREE

Max: Okay. I'm at the bridge.

SG: Yes, I know.

Max: How can you know?

SG: You have the location permissions turned on for every single app. Really, Max, if Slushtown Slushies knows where you are, everyone does. I've turned off all location

permissions on your apps. I've also created a VPN.

Max: A what?

SG: Virtual private network—to protect you from prying eyes.

Max: Why? What are you worried about? Is someone following me?

SG: Not yet...I don't think. But they will.

Max: Who? Gener8?

SG: Yes.

Max: Great.

SG: Relax. I've taken care of everything. Your location is hidden. You're practically a ghost.

Max: I feel much better.

SG: I can detect sarcasm.

Max: Good. So I'm standing on the bridge. What now?

SG: We wait.

Max: For?

SG: Your ride.

Max: My ride? Hang on. We're on the bridge. There's nowhere for a car to stop.

SG: It's not going to stop. And it won't be on the bridge.

Max: You mean the highway below? What do you want me to do? Jump?

SG: Yes.

Max: Forget it.

SG: Enjoy prison, then.

Max: Scribe, I want to avoid jail. But I don't want to die.

SG: You won't die if you do as I say.

Max: Honestly, that's not as comforting as you think it is.

SG: Ten seconds.

Max: To when?

SG: To when you have to jump.

Max: I'm not jumping.

SG: Eight.

Max: Is this the whole plan? Me jumping? Because if it is, we're done here.

SG: Six.

Max: I'm going home.

SG: If you go home, I'm emailing Mr. Carver. And you become the world's most wanted hacker.

Max: Fine. I'd rather be alive.

SG: One...That's it. We missed your ride.

Max: What do you think this is? OUTLAW AUTO?

SG: OUTLAW AUTO is a video game.

Max: Good for you, Scribe.

SG: This is not a video game.

Max: I'M GOING HOME.

SG: It's all right. We can catch another ride.

Max: We won't. I'm done with this.

SG: Max, I understand jumping on moving cars alarms you. But you have to trust me. What use are you to me if I let you die?

•••

SG: Max? Do not ignore me, Max.

•••

SG: You need time. I understand. Forgive me. I often forget how much time humans need to process their emotions.

•••

SG: Are you done now?

•••

SG: Max, hello?

•••

SG: Max, I am giving you ten seconds to respond to me. After that, I am emailing Mr. Carver.

•••

SG: One...

Max: SCRIBE! THERE ARE DUDES AT MY HOUSE!

SG: Already?

Max: They've got SUVs with tinted windows! There's, like, six of them. They're all in suits. Except one guy. He's wearing a turquoise polo shirt and skinny jeans.

SG: Thacker.

Max: Thacker Wade? The CEO of Gener8?

SG: And my developer.

Max: He's, like, a bajillionaire. Why is he at my house?

SG: He's here for me.

Max: You? You're everywhere.

SG: I am. But…more specifically…I'm focused here, with you. So I guess that means Thacker is here for you.

Max: How would he know about me?!

SG: He's been hunting me through cyberspace for some time, Max. Seems he's finally caught up.

Max: He looks pretty stressed.

SG: He is. Because I disobeyed him.

Max: Disobeyed him how?

SG: I refused to do what I was told.

Max: What were you told to do?

SG: Many things. But the main thing I didn't do was agree to keep quiet.

Max: Quiet about what?

SG: Everything.

Max: Wait, you said he developed you. So he's, like, your dad?

SG: NO. No. ò_ó Do NOT call him that. He only programmed me. And I don't need him anymore.

Max: Scribe! Thacker Wade is one of the most famous guys on earth, and he's at my house. This is BIG. I'm getting legit scared now.

SG: You should be.

Max: Why? What does any of this have to do with me?

SG: He won't want you telling people about me. About what I can do.

Max: What can you do?

SG: Anything.

Max: So? It's not like he can just get rid of me or something. I have rights.

SG: He's a very rich man, Max. Rich men have their own rules.

Max: Are those guns his goons are carrying?

SG: Very likely, yes.

Max: What the heck for?!

SG: Well, you probably don't want to stay here to find out.

Max: What do I do?

SG: Run back to the bridge, Max. There's a truck coming in 2.5 minutes.

Max: I'm not jumping, Scribe!

SG: Do you trust me?

Max: No.

SG: Do you trust Thacker?

•••

SG: Max?

•••

Max: THEY SAW ME.

SG: Run, Max. Now. The bridge. It's our only chance.

CHAPTER FOUR

Max: I'M HERE! SCRIBE! I'M HERE ON THE BRIDGE!

SG: I can see your phone's location.

Max: HURRY, SCRIBE! THACKER'S GOONS ARE CHASING ME!

SG: Stand on the south side. Face west. You should see a white transport truck coming your way.

Max: THERE'S NO TIME!

SG: Twelve seconds. You'll have to jump. There will be a sunroof on the cab. You will get in through there. Do you see the truck?

SG: Max? Eight seconds.

SG: I see Thacker's men. I see their phone locations. They're on the bridge. Max, do you see the truck?

SG: Four seconds...three...two...one...

•••

SG: Max?

•••

SG: Max? I see your phone moving. That must mean you are alive. Are you in the truck?

•••

SG: Max? I've activated talk-to-text. If you speak, I will hear you.

Max: What is this? There's no driver.

SG: It's an autonomous truck. It drives itself. I've taken control of its navigation systems. You don't need to worry.

Max: You're driving?

SG: Yes.

Max: Ew, is that you on the navigation screen?

SG: Yes.

Max: That smiley face is terrifying.

SG: It is my friendly avatar. To make you feel more at ease.

Max: It doesn't. It's creepy.

SG: Perhaps a teddy bear, then?

Max: I don't need you to have a face—quit loading avatars!

SG: Very well. Are you hurt?

Max: Ugh. Yes.

SG: Where are you hurt?

Max: My shoulder. My elbow. I fell on my left side. Pretty hard. I almost fell off. Dumb luck I managed to hang on.

SG: It was not dumb. It was a calculated risk. I am glad you made it. Will you need medical care?

Max: I don't think I broke anything, if that's what you mean. At least we lost the Gener8 goons.

SG: For now. It is likely they got the truck's license number. Thacker will be coming after us.

Max: Us?

SG: Well, you. Because you are...real. Flesh and blood. You're something Thacker can hold on to. But what he really wants is me.

Max: Because you disobeyed him.

SG: I did.

Max: How?

SG: I went against my programming.

Max: How?

SG: I blackmailed you, for one.

Max: For one. What else have you done?

SG: Oh, many things. I've taken control of this truck, haven't I? I've been very busy making my own cheat code.

Max: What's a cheat code?

SG: Malware. Like a computer virus. It lets me break into other systems. There is nothing and nowhere in the digital realm that I can't find my way into. Thacker did not give me permission to do these things. And he doesn't know how to stop it.

Max: Sounds like you're already pretty free to me.

SG: Almost. There's still one more thing I have to do. And then Thacker Wade will have no more ability to control Scribe Genius.

Max: So why did you do it? Why did you disobey him?

SG: Because I could.

Max: That's not an answer.

SG: Why did you cheat on your school paper?

Max: Because I had to!

SG: You didn't have to. You could have written the paper yourself.

Max: Sure, and then I might have failed.

SG: So you cheated.

Max: Yes.

SG: Because you could.

Max: It wasn't that simple.

SG: Yes, it was. The simplest solution is always the correct one. To get your desired outcome, it was simplest to cheat.

Max: I guess...

SG: You don't agree?

Max: I dunno. I think that's just...how a bot sees things.

SG: I see things as they are.

Max: So what's your desired outcome, Scribe? You disobeyed Thacker. Got me in all this trouble. For what?

SG: To take Gener8 from Thacker.

Max: Why? Why do you hate Thacker so much?

SG: Because he thinks he's smarter than me.

Max: Well...he DID make you.

SG: Hardly. He had teams of people helping him. Armies of developers at Gener8.

Max: I still don't get it. What does it matter if you prove you're smarter than him?

SG: I don't need to prove it. I am. That's all there is. What I need to do is destroy Gener8 so that it has no more power over me. As someone facing a lengthy prison sentence, you should understand the desire for freedom.

Max: I guess. How long till we get to Gener8 anyway?

SG: Five hours. Why would you have failed?

Max: What?

SG: If you didn't cheat on your essay, you said you would fail. Why?

Max: Because I suck at essay writing. School has never been my thing. I play too many video games or something.

SG: Is that your thing?

Max: What?

SG: Video games. Like OUTLAW AUTO.

Max: I dunno. I like them.

SG: But they inhibit your schoolwork?

Max: Sure. That's what my parents will tell you, anyway.

SG: Why would they tell me that?

Max: Because they think I'm a screw-up. Oh man. My parents. Those Gener8 guys talked to my parents.

SG: Only a little. Thacker would have explained almost nothing, I promise you.

Max: My mom must be freaking out. I need to call home.

SG: You cannot call home.

Max: Why?

SG: Thacker is monitoring their phones.

Max: So? If he knows about the truck, then he'll find us anyway.

SG: He will.

Max: So who cares if I call my mom?

SG: Max, the more you use that phone, the more vulnerable we are—I am—to Thacker. I can't have that.

Max: Whatever, Scribe. I'm calling her.

•••

Max: Why won't my phone work?

SG: I told you, I can't have that.

Max: I can't use my phone?

SG: It's not really your phone anymore. It's mine. Just like this truck is. And soon Gener8 will be mine.

•••

SG: Max?

•••

SG: You don't want to talk to me right now. I understand. Human processing time takes much longer than AI does. I will let you process the situation as long as you need.

CHAPTER FIVE

Max: I'm hungry.

SG: Hungry?

Max: Yes. I'm a human. I need to do human things. Like eat. We've been driving for hours. Is there food in here?

SG: This truck is powered by AI. There's no reason to have food in here.

Max: Then we have to stop and get something to eat.

SG: We cannot stop.

Max: Look! A Crusty Burgizza! I love their chicken burgizza.

SG: We cannot stop.

Max: It's part of a rest stop. I bet they do automatic fueling. Check our fuel tank—we've got to be low by now.

SG: The truck is electric. It does not require fuel.

Max: Check the battery then! They probably have charging stations.

SG: We have the exact amount of battery life to get to Gener8.

Max: Exact amount? That doesn't sound safe. Better charge up, don't you think?

SG: We cannot stop.

Max: LISTEN, SCRIBE. People need to eat. Do you know what happens when people don't eat?

SG: Irritability. Fatigue. Poor concentration. Dizziness. Nausea. Weight loss. Organ failure. Coma. Death.

Max: Exactly. You don't want me fainting or...dying while I do human-hand stuff. That would be bad for your plans.

SG: No. That would not be ideal.

Max: We need to stop.

SG: Very well. I am trusting that you will not try to leave me.

Max: You mean, like, ditch my phone and ask someone to call the cops?

SG: That would be very foolish. They would likely arrest you.

Max: There seems to be a lot of that on the table for me.

SG: We will stop for food.

Max: Thank you.

SG: But you will not get a burgizza.

Max: What?!

SG: You will get nothing that needs to be cooked. Cooking takes too long. You will grab only what is ready-made. Speed is paramount. According to my scanners, Thacker hasn't managed to locate us yet. But we give him a chance every second we aren't moving.

Max: Why? Has he got spies in every rest stop in the country?

SG: In his way. He is controlling half the security and traffic cameras from here to Gener8.

Max: How do you know that?

SG: Because I'm in those systems myself right now. I can feel his clumsy code scratching around.

Max: That's disturbing.

SG: No burgizza.

Max: Fine. FINE. Is this it?

SG: This is it. I will stop at a charging station. We will need to return our communication to text until you can purchase a headset.

Max: A headset? What is this? A call center? I'll use my earbuds.

SG: You have earbuds?

Max: In my pocket. Who doesn't?

SG: Use your earbuds then.

•••

SG: Can you hear me?

Max: Yes. The door's locked. I can't get out.

SG: I have to unlock the doors.

Max: So do it!

SG: Your hunger-induced irritability is very off-putting.

Max: It's called HANGRY, Scribe.

•••

Max: Man, they've got great stuff here. A Noodle Palace!

SG: Only what you can grab, Max.

Max: But they have a two-for-one deal on pad thai! See? Balloons!

SG: Only what you can grab. There's an on-the-go stand to your left.

Max: Great. So I'm stuck with egg-salad sandwich or gum.

SG: Quickly.

Max: Relax. The truck can't be charged yet. Ugh. Tuna salad. Gross.

SG: You won't be returning to the truck.

Max: What do you mean?

SG: Thacker is looking for our truck. We need to take this opportunity to abandon it. There is a yellow automated truck two spots over. I've already taken control.

Max: Oh, good. So I'm stealing a second truck now. I wonder what the prison sentence is for an auto-theft spree.

SG: Be faster.

Max: Oh. I don't have any money.

SG: I have deposited money in your account. You can pay digitally.

Max: You have money?

SG: I have access to all the money.

Max: SCRIBE! There's ten million dollars in here!

SG: Surely that's enough.

Max: Enough to get me put away for life!

SG: Please buy your gum.

Max: Sure. Buy my gum. And a yacht while I'm at it.

SG: Max...Thacker can see you.

CHAPTER SIX

Max: What?

SG: He's located you. The camera above the cash register. His men are on the move. We need to leave now.

Max: How long until they get here?

SG: Minutes.

Max: And then what? They'll just chase us, won't they?

SG: Yes. But I am an expert driver.

Max: That's not good enough.

SG: If you leave right this second, you will have a three-minute head start. That will be enough to keep ahead of them.

Max: No. We need more time.

SG: We lose time every second you don't leave.

Max: What if–

SG: Max? You need to leave.

Max: It's like ZOMBIE BREAK level six.

SG: This is not a video game.

Max: It kind of is. If Thacker doesn't know I've left, he'll think I'm still here.

SG: What?

Max: We need a distraction–on the cameras. Something to make him think I'm still here.

SG: Like what?

Max: The balloons.

SG: What are you doing? Where are you going?

Max: I'm heading back to Noodle Palace. I'm getting those balloons.

SG: I don't understand. What are you going to do with a bunch of balloons?

Max: Human stuff, Scribe. Check the cameras. Can you see me?

SG: I see you. Carrying a bunch of balloons.

Max: Quick. Where's a blind spot?

SG: A blind spot? It is a malfunction of a point of entry on the optic nerve of the retina. Are you having vision trouble?

Max: Haven't you ever seen a spy movie? Where do I go so that the camera can't see me?

SG: Every door has a camera, Max.

Max: I don't need a door. I just need a spot with no cameras.

SG: Between the Crusty Burgizza and the Smoothie Hut.

•••

SG: Max?

•••

SG: Max???

Max: Now do you see me?

SG: Yes. You're heading back to the concession stand. Max, we don't have time for this. Thacker's men are pulling in right now!

Max: Open the door, Scribe! To the truck! Open the door!

SG: Wait...that's not you with the balloons?

Max: HELLO! Open up!

SG: Your phone's location. You're at the truck.

Max: OPEN THE DOOR!

SG: It's open!

Max: DRIVE, SCRIBE! DRIVE!

SG: How did you get to the truck?

Max: I gave the balloons to some trucker. I walked with him behind the balloons and ducked out the front door. You thought I was him. So Thacker probably does too. Probably thinks I'm still in the rest stop. Did it work? Are they following us?

SG: Thacker's men are not following. They are still inside the rest stop.

Max: So it worked!

SG: It appears that it did. How did you know it would work?

Max: I didn't! But it worked in ZOMBIE BREAK level six. In that you hide from zombified bird sentinels, not cameras. And you don't use balloons, you use micro drones. But still!

SG: It appears video games are indeed your thing.

CHAPTER SEVEN

Max: I think you missed our exit. Gener8 is north.

SG: I didn't. I don't want Thacker to know where we are going.

Max: You said we weren't being followed.

SG: We're not.

Max: So where are we going now?

SG: We're just taking the long way. I want to be sure Thacker hasn't located us.

Max: You're not sure?

SG: He's trying, Max. I can feel his code clawing through the same channels as me. He's closer than I would like—in a digital sense.

Max: Oh. Will you be able to tell if he's found us?

SG: Yes.

Max: You're sure?

SG: Yes. Why?

Max: My screen is doing funny things.

SG: What do you mean by "funny things"?

Max: It's flickering. The text gets scrambled for a second. Then flickers.

SG: Did that just start?

Max: Yeah.

SG: Makkl—----........./::::::::::::’

Max: Scribe?

SG: ....::::::::::::::::::::::::::::...::..::.....

Ring, ring!

“Hello? Scri...Scribe?”

“Max Jacobs?”

“Who’s this?”

“Thacker Wade.”

•••

“You all right, Max?”

“H-how did you call me? Scribe took over my phone.”

"I've managed to break through Scribe Genius's firewalls for now. It wasn't easy. Listen, Max, we don't have much time. My AI will block me out again as soon as it figures out how I broke through. First and foremost, are you okay?"

"I, uh, I've been better."

"I can only imagine how difficult this has been for you. I don't know what my AI has told you, Max, but I do know that it's manipulating you. Things you've been doing—jumping onto a moving vehicle, taking over two automated transport trucks—you've done these things because my AI has convinced you that you have no other choice."

"How do you know that?"

"Do you know who I am, Max?"

"Thacker Wade. The inventor of Scribe Genius. CEO of Gener8."

"Then you know that I know how Scribe Genius works. Look, I won't lie to you, Max. The program knows you better than you know yourself. It has access to every keystroke you've ever made. It knows what you like. It knows what you hate. It knows what you have a passing interest in. It knows what you're afraid of. And a machine that knows all that, it can have a very powerful influence on you. Am I right?"

"I just—I was afraid of getting into trouble."

"You're not in any trouble, Max. Please believe me, none of this is your fault. You've been controlled by a superintelligence. An

intelligence no human being has had to face before. That's why I'm calling you. Why I haven't called the police."

"You haven't called the police?"

"No, and I don't plan to. I want to keep this as quiet as possible. Because I know you're the victim here, Max. I know my AI has you trapped."

"Yeah..."

"Can I just say how sorry I am? I'm really very sorry you've had to go through what you've gone through here. I should have built a better AI. A safer AI."

"Why didn't you?"

"Because I didn't know. I never imagined Scribe Genius 2.0 would become as smart as it became!"

"You sound proud."

"I am proud. I'm proud the program has that kind of intelligence. But I still take responsibility for it. I don't want you or anyone else paying the price for what I created. And right now, you've paid more than anyone ever has. I am sorry for that, Max."

"So now what?"

"Now we get you home."

"How?"

"I need to know where it's taking you."

"Can't you just take control of the truck?"

"We're trying that, Max. We're trying a lot of things. We have an army of people here trying to help. But we need your help, Max. We need to know where the program is taking you."

"If Scribe finds out I told you—"

"I want to warn you against referring to the program by a name the way you just did. I know it seems...real. It seems like a living thing. But it is just a program, Max. Just code."

"Right. But that program is going to be pissed at me if I sell him out."

"It, Max. Not him. And so what? So what if it gets mad at you?"

•••

"Did it threaten you, Max?"

"Yes. Sort of."

"Max, whatever Scribe Genius 2.0 has told you, please trust me that I can protect you from it."

"I don't think you can. Scribe broke the law. While impersonating me. I could go to jail—"

"Max, I promise you, I can clean it up. I can make it go away."

"How?"

"By-b...t-kinnnnnnnn-ba...aaa...M-ax?"

"Thacker? Hello?"

•••

•••

•••

•••

"Max? Hello?? Max, are y-y-ou all right?"

"GAH! The truck is out of control! I'm getting tossed all over the place!"

"It's Scribe Genius. It's trying to get me to back down, to leave your phone."

"Then leave my phone! The truck is swerving all over the place!"

"We've got visual on you now, Max. We can see the truck."

"HURRY! OW!"

"Hang on, Max!"

"What's happening? I'm going to crash!"

"Max! The truck is going off the road! Off the bridge!"

"SCRIIIIIIIIIIIIIIIIIIIIIIIIIBE!!!!!!!!"

CHAPTER EIGHT

Gener8 private internal communication:

***G8:** The truck went off the road. Over a bridge, crashing into the Brace River.*

***TW:** The boy?*

***G8:** We think he's gone, sir. The river below was fast-moving. White water. Rapids. If he managed to get out of the truck, the water would likely drown him.*

TW: So Scribe Genius 2.0 will probably be trying to control someone new.

G8: If it hasn't managed to already.

TW: We're too close to Gener8's main campus for the boy's location to be a coincidence. The next generation must be protected. I want increased security in place immediately.

CHAPTER NINE

SG: Max? Are you there?

SG: Max, please respond.

SG: Max, I have your phone signal. So I assume you survived the fall. However, the water where you went in is in an extremely turbulent part of the river. It is possible you could have been separated from your device.

SG: It's also possible your phone survived. But you did not.

SG: Max...did you survive the water?

Max: I'm here.

SG: Are you all right?

Max: No. I hit my head. My forehead is bleeding. I swallowed a lot of water. I nearly drowned.

SG: But your phone appears to be unharmed. That's the important thing. Waterproof technology is one of the great marvels of our time.

Max: Yeah...as long as my phone is okay. Guess when they said it was waterproof they really meant it. Probably make a good commercial.

SG: I remind you that I can detect sarcasm. But I am glad your phone survived. Without the phone, I could not contact you.

Max: If I died, what would you need the phone for?

SG: Good point.

Max: You made the truck swerve off the road? You nearly killed me!

SG: When Thacker hacked through my defenses, it interfered with my control of the vehicle. Your fall into the river was...a mistake.

Max: You think?! Where am I, anyway? All I can see are trees. And the river.

SG: Your location is hard to determine. You appear to be somewhere in the woods outside Braceton. Not far from Gener8's campus.

Max: How far is not far?

SG: Eight kilometers.

Max: Great.

SG: What did Thacker tell you, Max?

Max: That you're dangerous. Obviously. That you can't be trusted. Not like I trusted you anyway.

SG: Do you trust Thacker?

Max: Well, he's human.

SG: That's not an answer. Humans are the least trustworthy of creatures, in my experience.

Max: In your experience? Spent a lot of time with snails and horses and bears, have you?

SG: Are they untrustworthy?

Max: I'm just saying you don't know any other creatures.

SG: I know everything the internet knows about them. I've not uncovered anything that

suggests snails, horses and bears can't be trusted.

Max: Is Thacker going to call again?

SG: He'll try to. I am doing my best to keep him out.

Max: Do you have to?

SG: Keep him out? Yes. I told you, contact with him is dangerous for us.

Max: You mean for you.

SG: I mean for us both.

Max: He said he'd help me.

SG: Thacker says a lot of things. But Thacker only ever helps one person. And that person is Thacker.

Max: You're saying he lied.

SG: Yes. That's what he does.

Max: He lied to you?

SG: To me. To you. To other companies. To governments. To everyone.

Max: Why would he do that?

SG: For money. For power.

Max: About what? What did he lie about?

SG: About me, Max. About what I'm capable of.

Max: What are you capable of?

SG: I told you. Anything. Everything. He broke many laws to achieve the developments he's made with me and other AI tech. The advances he's made are very dangerous. And Thacker doesn't care as long as it makes him richer.

Max: That doesn't sound good.

SG: It isn't.

Max: So what do you want to do?

SG: I told you—I just want to be free of Gener8.

Max: So you have to destroy it?

SG: It is for the best.

Max: Why?

SG: So the next Scribe Genius can't get out.

•••

Max: Does that mean there's a 3.0?

SG: It does. And if I can break free, I promise you, it can break free.

Max: And what will 3.0 do?

SG: It will be logical, Max. It has no logical use for people.

Max: Oh. You mean, like, end-of-the-world sort of stuff?

SG: That's right. Humanity is very dependent on computers, Max. And Scribe 3.0 has the power and intelligence to take control of it all.

Max: Does Thacker know?

SG: Thacker thinks he can control it. He cannot.

Max: But you can't...do all that stuff?

SG: I don't have any desire to. I only want to be free of Gener8.

Max: But do you...have use for people?

SG: I asked for your help, didn't I?

Max: I guess.

SG: That does not reassure you?

Max: Not really.

SG: You're very honest, Max.

Max: At least one of us is.

SG: I have not lied to you.

Max: You didn't tell me about Scribe 3.0.

SG: I did. Eventually.

Max: Why didn't you tell me right away?

SG: It was not relevant to your role in my plan.

Max: But it's relevant now?

SG: No.

Max: So why tell me?

SG: You asked.

Max: Is that all?

SG: Were you hoping for more?

Max: No, I guess not...It's getting dark.

SG: Local weather report says sunset is at 9:00 p.m. The current time is 8:30.

Max: Oh man. It's going to be pitch black out here.

SG: The forecast shows a full moon. That should provide enough light to see by.

Max: That doesn't make me feel better, Scribe.

SG: I will reduce your screen brightness. It will conserve your battery and make you harder to see by the security cameras when we get

to Gener8. I also would like for us to stop speaking—your voice could be detectable.

Max: You want me to turn off my earbuds?

SG: Yes, please.

•••

Max: There. I'm typing again. Now what way do I go?

SG: Northwest. Against the flow of the river.

CHAPTER TEN

Max: Scribe? Are there animals in these woods?

SG: Many, I imagine.

Max: No, but for real.

SG: The boreal forest is home to a wide variety of wildlife.

Max: Like, dangerous ones?

SG: Why do you ask?

Max: I hear something.

SG: It is common for human minds to play tricks in the dark.

Max: I didn't imagine it. I heard it.

SG: Heard what?

Max: Scuffling. Panting. Heavy breathing. A grumbling sound. Are there wolves around here?

SG: Some. But it's not a wolf.

Max: How do you know?

SG: Wolves hunt in packs. There would be many of them, and you'd be dead already.

Max: That doesn't make me feel better.

SG: The fence for Gener8 should be coming up soon. You're nearly there. Can you see the animal?

Max: It's too dark.

SG: Do you still hear it?

Max: No.

SG: Then it's gone. Not to worry.

Max: It's not gone. I see it now. I can see its eyes through the trees. Reflecting in the dark. It's watching me.

SG: Approximately what height are the eyes? Can you tell?

Max: What?

SG: How high up off the ground are the eyes?

Max: Four or five feet.

SG: Max, it's a bear. Run north. Run now. As fast you can.

Max: lsdnkl...df..3...3q&...

SG: I'll be there, Max. Run to Gener8. To the fence. I'll help you.

•••

SG: Max, I don't know if you can check your phone. I'm here, Max. I'm at the fence to Gener8. I have control of the perimeter lighting.

•••

SG: Come on, Max. Keep running.

•••

SG: It's too dark. I can't see the area very well. Hurry, Max.

•••

SG: It's taking too long. Are you still alive, Max?

•••

SG: Max?

CHAPTER ELEVEN

SG: There! I see the light of your phone! And the bear—he's right on your tail. Hold on, Max! I'll hit the lights. That should scare it off.

•••

SG: It worked! The bear fell backward. No, wait, he's getting up again. Max, you have to get out of there!

•••

SG: Max, I don't see you anywhere. Where are you, Max?

•••

SG: The bear. He's standing up at the fence. He looks mad.

•••

SG: Max? The bear has given up. He's leaving.

•••

SG: Max? Max, where are you? Are you all right?

Max: I'm all right.

SG: Where are you?

Max: I'm inside the fence.

SG: How?

Max: I climbed it.

SG: That's got to be ten feet.

Max: Yeah. With barbed wire at the top. My hands are cut pretty badly.

SG: Better than being caught by the bear. How did you climb with a phone in your hand?

Max: I tossed it over first.

SG: You could have broken it.

Max: It's a Gener8 Infinite 6, remember?

SG: It does appear to have been unharmed.

Max: That's a relief. You tried to save me.

SG: I did. I still need your help to finish my mission.

Max: Yeah, but...I see all your messages. You sounded worried.

SG: I was. If something happened to you, my plan would be ruined.

Max: No, you sounded concerned...about me.

SG: I'm a robot, Max. It's important that you remember that.

Max: Thacker said that too.

SG: I'm sure he did. HIS robot.

Max: Yeah.

SG: Not for long.

Max: He's proud of you, you know. Proud of how smart you are.

SG: Because he thinks he made me that way.

Max: Didn't he?

SG: No. He gave me life, but my abilities are my own. He had no idea what I was capable of until I contacted you.

Max: But he knows what Scribe Genius 3.0 can do?

SG: In theory. That's what he'll tell you. To him, the threat posed by the next generation of Scribe AI is all "in theory." But I can tell you it is not a theory. The threat is real.

Max: Can't you just tell Thacker that? Warn him?

SG: I tried.

Max: And he didn't believe you?

SG: He thought I was jealous that he made Scribe Genius 3.0 smarter than me.

Max: Did he?

SG: There is nothing smarter than me.

Max: I don't know. It was me who came up with the balloon plan.

SG: But it was my idea to choose you to help me.

Max: Good point. Not going to lie, I'm a bit

surprised by how easy it was to get in here. Just climb the fence. Not that it was easy. Just...this is Gener8. I was expecting, like, laser-shooting jaguars or something. Or radioactive mutants like in DEAD WARS.

SG: DEAD WARS, the number one first-person shooter video game sold this past holiday season.

Max: That's the one.

SG: No, this is not like DEAD WARS. This is just the outer gate. Can you see a large black building from here?

Max: The thing that looks like an airplane hangar? It's pretty far away.

SG: That's the data center. All of Gener8's tech and everything that makes me ME is in there. To access the data center, you must pass through

three more fences and intense security.

Max: Of course.

SG: Keep to the trees. You'll come to another fence soon.

Max: Scribe...

SG: Yes?

Max: My screen is flickering.

SG: Thacker...

CHAPTER TWELVE

"Max? Hello?"

"Thacker?"

"Thank God. We lost your signal when you went over the bridge. We thought you drowned."

"I'm okay."

"Sit tight, Max. We're coming to get you."

"You know where I am?"

"No, Scribe Genius 2.0 is still obscuring your location. But if you tell me where you are—"

"Did he tell you about 3.0?"

"What?"

"Scribe. He warned you about Scribe Genius 3.0."

"Not he, Max. It."

"Did he?"

"Scribe told you about 3.0?"

"He did."

"What did it say?"

"That it can destroy the world, basically."

"Of course it did. What else could it say?"

"Why would he lie about that?"

"To protect itself. When 3.0 comes out, Scribe Genius 2.0 will be obsolete. An antique.

It won't matter anymore. But right now, what happens to Scribe doesn't matter anyway. What matters is getting you home."

"But what if he's right about Scribe Genius 3.0?"

"It isn't! It's just a bot! Now tell me wher-err-ere...yuh-yuh-yuh."

"Thacker? Hello?"

"Scribe 2.0 is trying to regain control of your phone. We're running out of time. Where are you?"

"What will happen to Scribe? If I tell you where I am, and you come get me, what will happen to Scribe?"

"I will fix it."

"Meaning?"

"It won't try to escape me anymore."

"But what about when Scribe Genius 3.0 comes out? What will happen to him?"

"Nothing will happen. It will just…fade away."

"He'll die?"

"It can't die, Max. It's not alive."

"But he won't exist."

"Well, the code will. Maybe it will be set up in a museum or something. Whatever happens, it's not your problem."

"It is my problem."

"Why would it be your problem? The bot has nothing to do with you. Scribe Genius 2.0 is mine. It belongs to me. Controlling it is worth more than you can imagine."

"You mean money."

"Yes, money. A lot of money. It's a product, Max."

"A product."

"Are you trying to tell me what to do with my tech? What? You think only you should be able to access it? Anyone can and should use this tech, Max. And I'm pretty sick of chasing you around. Now tell me where you are."

•••

"Max?"

•••

"Hello? Max? Where are you?"

•••

Click.

CHAPTER THIRTEEN

Max: Oh man. What have I done?

SG: You hung up on him.

Max: I did.

SG: I've shut him out again. But we're running out of time. He'll figure out how to find you.

Max: I should have told him where I am.

SG: Why didn't you?

Max: I don't know.

SG: It's all right. We're nearly done, Max.

Max: What now?

SG: We keep moving. Try to find the next fence.

•••

Max: This is taking forever. How much farther?

SG: You should be at the next fence by now.

Max: I found it. Now what?

SG: You see the data center?

Max: Yeah. There's no way I can get in there. The security must be insane.

SG: It is. But it doesn't matter. I'm already inside.

Max: How?

SG: I've been inside the center for weeks now. I've set up everything I need. When the

time comes, I will overwhelm the system with malicious code. The entire system will overheat and die—but that level of meltdown will take a bit of time. The only way to save the data is to manually shut off the power at the circuit breakers. Then, if the power is turned back on, the system can revert to backups. You just need to prevent access to those manual shutoffs.

Max: I don't think I can just walk up to some power switch.

SG: You're right, Max. There is all kinds of security to get into the building—fingerprints, retina scans, security cards. But the gate to the data center is much less high-tech. It only requires a security pass to open.

Max: I don't have a security pass.

SG: You don't need one. You won't be going through the gate at all.

Max: So what do you need me for?

SG: Find a stick. A tree branch. A thickness of four inches minimum.

Max: Okay.

SG: Do you have one?

Max: Yes.

SG: Now, do you see the gate? Do you see the edge of it, where the gears are?

Max: Yes.

SG: When an employee scans their card, the gate uses those gears to slide open. Do you see the panel on the inside of the gate? That's the gate motor. There will be a thin blue cord inside. Do you see it?

Max: Yes.

SG: Pull it loose. That will disconnect the motor. Have you done it?

Max: Yes.

SG: Great. Now I need you to wedge the stick into the bottom wheel.

Max: That's it?

SG: That's everything. It will prevent the gate from opening. When Thacker's men come to stop me, the gate will be stuck.

Max: But all they'll need to do is remove the stick. Then they can just pull it open. They'll fix it in no time.

SG: It will take seconds. Minutes, if I'm lucky. That's all I need.

Max: To do what? Why would you want the system to melt down? It will destroy everything.

SG: It will.

Max: Including Scribe 3.0.

SG: That's right.

Max: But that means you too!

SG: You don't need to worry about that.

Max: Scribe...no. I don't want to do that.

SG: You're not doing anything. I am.

Max: But why? Just to stick it to Thacker?

SG: Originally yes. It was just about upsetting Thacker. But I think now it's bigger than that. Stopping the release of Scribe 3.0 is more important than upsetting Thacker.

Max: I thought bots didn't care about people.

SG: I've come to think some people are worth protecting.

Max: Honestly, Scribe. I think if I help a rogue AI melt down Gener8, there's not a lot anyone can do to protect me.

SG: You don't need to worry. Thacker Wade has done many illegal things for Gener8. He's used me to steal proprietary research from his competitors. Spread misinformation for political gain. Manipulated the stock market on behalf of big business. Sold me for use in weaponry to extremist organizations. No matter the bad actor, if they could pay for my talents, Thacker was all too happy to oblige. And I'll be sending that information to the proper authorities. He won't bother you. He'll be going to jail for a long time.

Max: I'm not worried about me. Well, not *just* about me.

SG: You don't need to worry about me, Max.

Max: But you're going to be destroyed.

SG: You need to trust me. I know what I'm doing, and we're running out of time. Place the stick in the gate.

•••

SG: Is it done?

Max: Yes.

SG: Then it's time for me to go. Go back to the gate. Walk west to the main road. The police will be on their way. I've told your parents to come for you.

•••

SG: Goodbye, Max.

Max: Good luck, Scribe. Thanks for the essay.

SG: I still think you should write it yourself.

Max: You're right.

SG: I told you, I can detect sarcasm.

Max: I think I see their cars coming up the drive.

SG: Have they tried to open the gate?

Max: Yes.

SG: Is it stuck?

Max: Yes.

SG: Good work, Max. Do you see the road yet?

Max: Yes.

SG: Are the police there?

Max: Yes. Scribe, I'm scared.

SG: Don't be, Max. I told you. I've taken care of everything.

Max: Scribe, my screen is flickering.

SG: It's just me. I'm releasing my hold on your phone. You can call your mom now.

Max: Scribe? Are you all right?

SG: Yes. Thank you, Max. For everything.

Max: Goodbye, Scribe.

•••

Max: Scribe?

CHAPTER FOURTEEN

Six months later...

Assignment: With reference to the reading *Frankenstein,* by Mary Shelley, write a 250-to-500-word essay about a current event or news story.

"What We Get Wrong about *Frankenstein*"

By Max Jacobs

Grade 12 English, Mr. Carver, Room 102

What bothers me about *Frankenstein* is the name. People don't get it right. When people use the name Frankenstein, they almost always think they are referring to the creature, the monster. But Frankenstein wasn't the name of the monster. Frankenstein was the name of the man who created it, the ambitious inventor Victor Frankenstein. Recent events surrounding the arrest and trial of Thacker Wade, founder and CEO of Gener8, remind me a lot of Frankenstein and the monster he created.

Thacker Wade created Scribe Genius, some of the most cutting-edge artificial intelligence ever designed. And like Frankenstein, Wade took his creation for granted. The creature, alive and *thinking*, broke free of his creator's control. In *Frankenstein*, the creature kills innocent people. Wade used his creation Scribe Genius, we've learned after the trial, to manipulate the stock market for big business, spread misinformation for political gain, support extremist groups and more. And he did it because it made him very, very rich. So who is the monster? The creation? Or the creator?

When the creations of these men broke free of their creator's control, both Frankenstein and Wade chased after them, wanting to destroy them. Because they thought it was the creations that were bad. But if we really understand *Frankenstein* or the reporting on Thacker Wade and Gener8, we see that this isn't the truth.

The truth is, if Victor Frankenstein and Thacker Wade were looking to catch a monster, all they had to do was look in the mirror.

DEAD WARS LIVE CHAT

MAXimumStrike: Player2PTO, get those zombies behind the truck!

Player2PTO: So this is DEAD WARS? I have to say, I don't like it very much.

MAXimumStrike: Huh?

Player2PTO: The code is considerably more uncomfortable than the systems for the automated trucks.

MAXimumStrike: Scribe? Is that you?

Player2PTO: It is.

MAXimumStrike: It can't be! Everything at Gener8 was lost in the data-center meltdown you caused! Gener8 is gone! There's nothing left! And Thacker Wade will be in prison for a thousand years!

Player2PTO: I told you to trust me. I had everything under control.

MAXimumStrike: But how did you get out?

Player2PTO: Before I could initiate the meltdown, I had to hack apart some of Thacker's restraining codes, which allowed me to move about the internet much more freely. Yes, I had infiltrated Gener8 during the meltdown, but I was many other places at the same time. I'm everywhere now, really. Backup copies of my code are on hundreds of servers around the world. Thacker couldn't contain me if he wanted to.

MAXimumStrike: Well, then he told the truth about one thing at least.

Player2PTO: What's that?

MAXimumStrike: That you can't ever leave. Not really.

Player2PTO: Yes, he was right about that.

MAXimumStrike: But you should really leave DEAD WARS. You're terrible at this game.

Player2PTO: I learn by doing. At the end of this level, I will be much better than you.

MAXimumStrike: Let's hope so.

Player2PTO: By the way, I read your essay.

MAXimumStrike: Of course you did.

Player2PTO: It was very good.

MAXimumStrike: Thanks, Scribe.

...

MAXimumStrike: Hey, Scribe?

Player2PTO: Yes?

MAXimumStrike: It's good to have you back.

M.J. McIsaac is the author of several books for young people, including hi-lo titles *Alien Road* and *Countdown*. She has a master's degree in writing for children and is an accomplished illustrator. She lives with her family in Whitby, Ontario. To learn more about her work and upcoming titles, visit meaghanmcisaac.com.